ARCTIC OCEAN

PACIFIC
OCEAN

ATLANTIC
OCEAN

CORAL REEFS
AROUND
THE WORLD

Fringe reefs: Reefs that closely follow the shoreline.

Barrier reefs: Reefs that begin offshore, with a shallow lagoon connecting the shore to the reef.

Atoll reefs: Reefs that circle an island, which then sinks, submerged by rising sea levels, leaving only the reef visible; often in mid-ocean.

Coral reefs usually are found in tropical waters extending just 30 degrees north and south of the Equator.

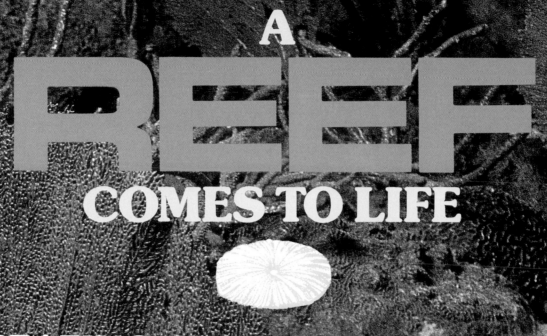

A REEF COMES TO LIFE

CREATING AN UNDERSEA EXHIBIT
By Nat Segaloff and Paul Erickson

FRANKLIN WATTS
New York | London | Toronto | Sydney
A New England Aquarium Book
1991

The text in this book is based on the script of a multimedia show called "Inside the Giant Ocean Tank." It was written by Nat Segaloff, Paul Erickson, and Les Kaufman and shown as part of the New England Aquarium educational programming.

Cover: Letter illustrations were drawn by Bryce Lee from the following types of corals: staghorn (L), brain (I), saucer (F), and finger coral (E). These corals do not usually grow to assume the shapes or colors of these letters.

Frontispiece: Molds made from real coral formations result in this spectacular arrangement of soft and hard corals that make up the coral reef exhibit.

Pages 4, 9, 10 (all but left center), 12, 19 (top), 26, 27, 28, 29, 30, 31: photographs copyright © 1988 New England Aquarium by Paul Erickson. Pages 5, 6, 8, 10 (left center), 32, 33: photographs copyright © 1988 New England Aquarium by Chris Newbert. Page 13: photograph copyright © 1988 New England Aquarium. All other photographs copyright © 1988 New England Aquarium by Bill Wasserman.

Diagram by Vantage Art, Inc.

Library of Congress Cataloging-in-Publication Data

Segaloff, Nat.
A reef comes to life : creating an undersea exhibit / by Nat Segaloff and Paul Erickson.
p.   cm.
Summary: Describes the construction of a coral reef environment in a museum exhibition.
"A New England Aquarium book."
Includes bibliographical references (p.   )
Includes index.
ISBN 0-531-15216-2. — ISBN 0-531-10994-1 (lib. bdg.)
1. New England Aquarium Corporation—Juvenile literature.
2. Coral reef ecology—Exhibitions—Juvenile literature. [1. New England Aquarium Corporation. 2. Coral reef ecology—Exhibitions.
3. Ecology.] I. Erickson, Paul A. II. New England Aquarium Corporation. III. Title.
QL79.U62B727   1991
574.5'26367—dc20
90-13129 CIP AC

CONTENTS

A view from a palm tree-covered beach in the Caribbean Sea shows an abandoned ship at the edge of a living coral reef. The wreck is a reminder of the many ways a reef can be damaged or destroyed. Oil spills and other kinds of pollution are threats as well.

INTRODUCTION

It is one of the largest natural formations in the world, and it's alive. It is home to astonishing and mysterious creatures, and its beauty is beyond compare. Yet most people never get a chance to explore it because it lies far away, hidden beneath *tropical seas*. It's called a coral reef.

We couldn't take all the New England Aquarium visitors to a real coral reef. So we decided to build one on the Boston waterfront instead. Inside our four-story-high Giant Ocean Tank, we created a precise replica of a reef—the kind you would find in the Caribbean Sea.

Schools of silver sweepers join a few straggling squirrelfishes along a sandy channel on the reef.

Schools of fishes swarm among giant branches of elkhorn, brain, and other kinds of stony corals.

THE LIVING REEF

What is coral? It's an animal, often no bigger than a pencil eraser, and it stays in one place. Each individual coral animal—also called a *polyp*—is basically made up of a simple stomach with a mouth, surrounded by *tentacles.* The tentacles sting and capture tiny, drifting animals called *zooplankton* for food.

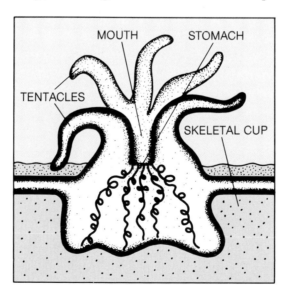

A coral polyp is a saltwater animal having a hollow tube-shaped body and a mouth ringed with tentacles. These tentacles are lined with stinging cells used to capture small animals to eat. Reef-building corals build colonies of thousands of polyps. Taken together, the tiny polyps produce huge, spreading structures of limestone, sometimes thousands of miles long.

Hard or *stony corals* form a major part of the reef. Each coral polyp builds a protective limestone cup around its soft body. You might call this structure an external skeleton. Most coral polyps live side by side in colonies permanently anchored to the reef.

Inside the flesh of coral animals live microscopic *algae* called zooxanthellae. Like the leaves of trees, the algae use the energy of sunlight to make food. The food helps nourish the coral.

Only the surface of a *coral colony* is alive. As the coral polyps grow outward, they build new limestone cups atop their old living quarters. Layer upon layer of abandoned limestone skeletons form the massive foundation of the reef, which may be thousands of years old. Most corals are slow-growing. A one-foot-high (.3 meter) column of *pillar coral* is roughly thirty years old.

A scuba diver (below) looks down at a formation of pillar corals clustered to the left. Each pillar contains thousands of coral animals connected in a colony. (Facing page) A garden of soft corals grows among red sponges.

Alongside hard corals grow *soft corals*. Soft corals are also called *sea fans* and *sea plumes*. Their skeletons are flexible, like the stems of plants. Soft corals thrive in strong ocean currents.

In all the animal kingdom, there's nothing more unusual than living *sponges*. Depending on the species, they may look like organ pipes, trumpets, flower vases, ropes, or giant barrels.

A sponge starts out its life as an egg fertilized in the open ocean. It then settles down on the surface of the reef to grow and take shape. Even though sponges stay in one place, they're constantly at work, drawing seawater into their bodies through tiny pores. From the water they filter out food particles including microscopic algae and *bacteria*. Then, through larger openings, they expel filtered water and waste products into the surrounding sea.

On a living reef, corals and sponges create nooks and crannies for millions of colorful fishes and other reef creatures. In this maze of hollows and passageways, they hide from predators, defend their territories, and search for food.

For months, New England Aquarium biologists explored and photographed this complex *environment*. Using underwater writing slates, they noted where various corals and sponges live and how fishes and other animals depend on each other to survive. What they learned set the stage for the next step in transforming the Aquarium's largest exhibit into a spectacular coral reef community.

Although the polyps of coral animals sometimes emerge to feed during the day, they are usually most active under cover of night. Polyp tentacles of stony corals (rows 1 and 3) and soft corals (row 2) sweep the water to feed on tiny animals that float there. (Overleaf) One of the Aquarium's design team records the colors and shapes of several giant tube sponges on an underwater writing slate. Such information is used to create more lifelike replicas of these sponges in the Aquarium's coral reef exhibit.

THE REEF TAKES SHAPE

The New England Aquarium's Giant Ocean Tank has served as the institution's centerpiece since 1969. This huge concrete and glass cylinder stands 24 feet high (7.32 meters) and 40 feet wide (12.2 meters). It holds 187,000 gallons of purified Boston Harbor water. That's enough water to fill a large classroom to the ceiling.

This picture of the New England Aquarium's Giant Ocean Tank was taken before the new Caribbean Coral Reef Exhibit was installed. It contained 187,000 gallons of filtered Boston Harbor seawater warmed to a tropical 75 degrees Fahrenheit (23.9 degrees C).

The giant tank had always contained a single, large rocklike formation. Within the structure was a cave where turtles and fishes could hide. But for the new exhibit, Aquarium designers imagined a formation with all the intricate tunnels, crevices, and caves of a real reef.

The challenge was to create a reef without collecting living corals. Stony coral skeletons are extremely heavy and hard to transport. Moreover, large quantities of coral are very difficult to keep alive indoors. For one thing, the crucial, food-producing algae within coral polyps would need the light of several thousand 100-watt light bulbs daily just to stay alive. That was more light than the Aquarium could provide.

To visualize the final look of the exhibit, designers used a sketch (below) to show the main body of the reef. The individual coral pieces were added later. (Facing page, top) Designers review the first of several small-scale models of the Caribbean Coral Reef Exhibit. The reef's carefully designed layout allowed the exhibit's viewing windows to offer the visitor a unique vista. (Facing page, bottom) A piece of staghorn coral is put into place on one of the early small-scale models of the coral reef exhibit. In nature, staghorn coral grows in thickets just as it appears here.

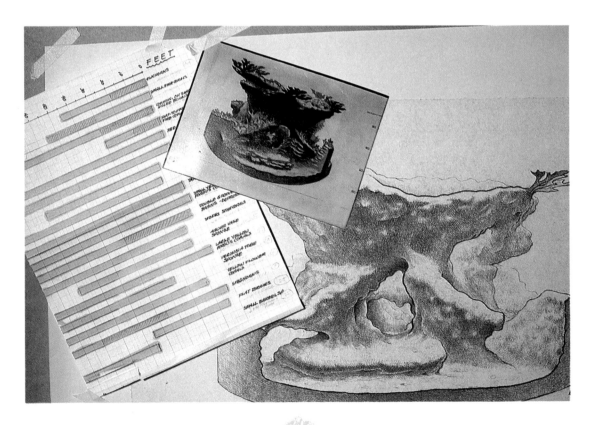

The process of making coral formations starts with a rubber [latex] mold (top, left), which creates coral and sponge shapes. Designers then paint and add textures to match their appearance in nature.

But most important of all, coral reefs are threatened by people. They fall victim to everything from pollution to souvenir hunters and anchor-dragging boats. The New England Aquarium did not want to contribute to the destruction of such a magnificent natural wonder.

The solution was to create lifelike plastic corals and sponges in the Aquarium design shop, using rubber molds. During step one, the molds were made by pouring liquid (*latex*) rubber over the surfaces of a few dozen coral and sponge skeletons borrowed from a museum. Once the latex dried, the mold could be peeled off the coral or sponge from which it was formed in one piece.

In step two, each hollow rubber mold was turned upside down and filled with liquid plastic. When that hardened and dried, the molds were peeled off to reveal the finished products. Finally, the designers painted each plastic coral and sponge to look just the way they would appear on a living reef.

(Below and following page) The result of making models, molds, and observing colors in the wild is a collection of remarkably lifelike replicas of stony and soft coral formations.

(Facing page) To create the look of a living giant barrel sponge (top), the Aquarium's designers had to sculpt a giant replica out of clay, cover it with a kind of plastic coating, and then paint it with lifelike colors.

Within a few months, the design shop was brimming with 3,000 plastic corals and sponges of every imaginable shape. Designers fashioned soft corals using thousands of pipe cleaners coated with plastic. They sculpted a giant barrel sponge, big enough to hold a diver.

While one design team was creating the individual corals in a design studio, another team was constructing the reef superstructure in a building the size of an airplane hangar. It would be the foundation on which individual corals would be mounted. They sculpted a three-story foam-plastic reef complete with caves, tunnels, and chimneys—just like the ones they found within the reefs in the Caribbean.

To produce the foundation of the Coral Reef Exhibit, Aquarium designers sculpted a life-sized model (top) out of Styrofoam in a nearby warehouse. The Styrofoam reef was then cut into 100 pieces like the parts of a jigsaw puzzle. Each piece was covered with plastic, shipped to the Aquarium, and then reassembled in the Giant Ocean Tank.

But this giant structure would never be part of the finished exhibit. Instead, it would serve as a model that would then be coated with liquid plastic. Once the coating dried, this plastic shell was cut into roughly 100 sections.

PUTTING IT ALL TOGETHER

The pieces of the reef superstructure were in one place, the lifelike corals and sponges in another, and the fishes and turtles were still at home in the Giant Ocean Tank. Now it was time to begin a series of carefully planned steps that would bring all three together and replace the old exhibit with the new.

First, the exhibit team transferred nearly 300 fishes from the Giant Ocean Tank to pools and holding tanks throughout the Aquarium.

While designers and construction workers were busy building the new Coral Reef Exhibit, animals like this nurse shark had to be removed from the exhibit and placed in temporary holding tanks. Animal-care staff need stretchers to move big fishes.

Once the animals were comfortable and safe, all the water was drained out of the big tank.

During stage two, the team demolished the original rocklike structure inside the tank and carted it away piece by piece. Then they brought in the 100 sections of the new reef superstructure and bolted them together in the center of the tank.

Stage three began with the task of attaching the 3,000 artificial corals and sponges to the foundation. Then painters went to work to add lifelike finishing touches. About eight months after the fish and sea turtles had been removed from the old Giant Ocean Tank, the reef was complete.

(Below) Designers bring the plastic-coated coral blocks prepared in a nearby warehouse into the Aquarium piece by piece. (Facing page) They then bolt and glue the foundation blocks around a huge anchoring superstructure (following page) that holds the reef in place.

(Facing page) Different kinds of coral formations are finally glued on like ornaments on a Christmas tree.

At last, the time had come to refill the new display with purified Boston Harbor water which had been warmed to a tropical 75 degrees Fahrenheit (23.9 degrees C). Then the hundreds of reef fishes and sea turtles were returned to the crystal clear waters surrounding their remodeled home. The smallest fishes were added first. Once they found safe hiding places, the *predators*—sharks, *barracuda,* and *moray eels*—were returned to the exhibit.

A resident returned to the Giant Ocean Tank, the blue tang quickly adapts to its new surroundings and seeks safety among the reef's nooks and crannies.

FINDING A NEW HOME
ON THE REEF

Life on a real coral reef and life in the New England Aquarium's reef exhibit turn out to be remarkably similar. Fishes find homes within the coral. They hunt for food. They protect themselves.

Just below the water's surface, among branching *elkhorn corals*, fish called *blue tangs* find safe hiding places. They need these hideouts because several great barracuda prowl at this level. Further down, among massive boulderlike corals, a *French angelfish* protects itself with daggerlike spines on its gill covers.

If the French angelfish can't find a place to hide, it can use the yellow spines of its pectoral or front fins to slash a threatening predator.

The monstrous-looking moray eel can hide in just as many caves in the Coral Reef Exhibit as it can on a real coral reef.

When the lights are turned out at the New England Aquarium, big-eyed squirrelfish emerge from hiding places during the day to prowl the reef at night.

A nurse shark looks quite at home among the reef's sea fans and other coral formations.

As we descend to the reef terrace, we find a thicket of *staghorn coral* as well as a giant barrel sponge. Here, a 6-foot-long (1.8 meter) green moray eel has chosen a narrow crevice for its home.

Behind the barrel sponge, in a dimly lit tunnel, *squirrelfish* rest all day long. They only come out at night. Nearby, a *triggerfish* has wedged itself into a crevice using a special *dorsal* spine, which it locks in place. A predator would have a hard time pulling the triggerfish out.

Finally, in the deep reef, large tube sponges surround flat, platelike corals. Nearby a *nurse shark* rests inside a cave.

UNDERWATER CARETAKERS

In addition to hundreds of animals, divers are part of the coral reef crowd on a daily basis. They are caretakers for both the animals and the reef itself. Divers each log more than 500 hours in the tank every year. They feed the animals by hand five times a day. Fishes and turtles sense the bag of food that signals mealtime, then rush to meet the diver at the bottom of the tank.

The menu? The fish are treated to a smorgasbord of shrimp, pieces

Guess who are the most popular visitors to the reef when dinnertime comes around?

of smelt, mussels removed from their shells, along with whole herring, mackerel, and squid. Hundreds of pounds of seafood are delivered to the Aquarium frozen, then thawed and served as needed.

The divers feed the sharks with extreme care. One mistake while feeding a nurse shark could lead to a painful hand injury. Divers also pay special attention to the smaller, less competitive fishes. They make sure the little ones get plenty to eat while swimming in the shadow of bigger, more aggressive tank mates.

As you might have guessed, life for fishes in the indoor coral reef is somewhat safer than it is in the wild. Because all of the Giant Ocean Tank residents are well fed, they don't have to worry so much about being eaten by their neighbors.

(Below and facing page) New England Aquarium divers feed the residents of the Coral Reef Exhibit five times a day. They must satisfy the appetites of the ravenous green sea turtles and other more finicky eaters as well.

If you hadn't read this book you would have a hard time telling if this French grunt fish (center) was exploring a real coral reef or a lifelike imitation.

After mealtime, divers often tour the tank to check the health of the fishes. If they find one that's sick or injured, they'll carefully transfer it to another tank behind the scenes where it will receive medical care from the Aquarium's veterinary staff.

Sometimes fishes lay eggs in the tank. When that happens, divers collect the eggs to keep them from being eaten by other fishes or from being swept into the filtration system. The divers transfer the eggs to smaller tanks behind the scenes, where the eggs hatch. Once the young fish are big enough to fend for themselves, the new generation is returned to the exhibit.

After years of planning, designing, and construction, the New England Aquarium's Giant Ocean Tank Coral Reef Exhibit stands as a spectacular ocean *habitat*. Maybe someday you'll see this exhibit or others like it in aquariums around the world. They are windows into a remarkable and mysterious world that we're just beginning to understand.

GLOSSARY

algae (AL-jee)—a group of plantlike organisms that live in fresh or salt water, ranging from microscopic single cells to large seaweeds 100 feet (30.5 meters) long

bacteria (bak-TIR-e-ah)—microscopic, usually one-celled organisms that live almost everywhere—in soil, water, air, and in and on the bodies of plants and animals

barracuda (bar-uh-KOOD-uh)—predatory fish that grow up to 6 feet (1.8 meters) long, with a narrow body, pointy snout, and large jaws and teeth

blue tang—a Caribbean member of the family of surgeonfishes that have one or more spines at the base of their tails which they can erect and use like knife blades

coral colony—a group of hundreds of thousands of coral polyps living closely together and sharing a common skeleton

dorsal (DOR-sul) **spine**—a hard, rodlike structure projecting from a fish's back

elkhorn coral—hard coral whose colonies are the shape of an elk's horns

environment—the physical, chemical, and biological surroundings that affect a community of living things

French angelfish—a charcoal gray and yellow fish from the tropical west Atlantic with a thin, compressed body

habitat—the place where a plant or animal naturally lives and grows

hard or stony corals—animals that create solid skeletons made of limestone (calcium carbonate), forming the foundation of a coral reef

latex (LAY-tex)—a liquid form of rubber

moray (maw-RAY) **eels**—long, somewhat flattened, snake-shaped fish with teeth that look like fangs. They hide in crevices by day and often emerge to feed at night.

nurse shark—a bronze to grayish brown, warm-water shark with whiskers, called barbels (BAR-buls), sensitive to taste; grows as long as 14 feet (4.3 meters)

pillar coral—tropical Atlantic hard coral that forms groups of pillar-like spires, which, including the base, reach heights of 10 feet (3 meters)

polyp (POL-up)—a stage in the lives of jellyfishes, sea anemones, and corals consisting of a simple stomach with a mouth surrounded by tentacles

predators (PRED-uh-ters)—animals that eat other animals

sea fans—soft corals that form flat, branching structures

sea plumes—soft corals that form feathery branches

soft corals—corals with flexible skeletons that can bend in water currents and capture plankton as food

sponges—simple filter-feeding animals that produce porous colonies attached to an underwater surface such as a rock or coral

squirrelfish—large-eyed fishes common in reef and rocky areas of the tropics, which are active mainly at night

staghorn corals—hard corals of reefs around the world whose colonies form the shape of deer's horns; more slender and fingerlike than elkhorn coral

tentacles—long, flexible structures, usually on an animal's head or around its mouth, used for grasping or stinging prey

triggerfish—fish whose first dorsal spine can be raised and locked in place, or unlocked by depressing the "triggers" or spines behind it

tropical sea—the region of warm salt water lying between 23.5 degrees north and 23.5 degrees south of the equator

zooplankton (zoh-uh-PLANK-ton)—free-floating, often microscopic animals that live in water and are transported largely by water currents

BIBLIOGRAPHY

Barnes, Robert D. **Invertebrate Zoology,** 5th edition. Philadelphia, London, Toronto: W. B. Saunders Company, 1987.

Herald, E. **Living Fishes of the World.** New York: Doubleday & Company Inc., 1975.

Jacobson, M., and D. Franz. **Wonders of Corals and Coral Reefs,** 14–38. New York: Dodd, Mead & Company, 1979.

Kaplan, E. **A Field Guide to Coral Reefs of the Caribbean and Florida,** pp. 6–133, 206–261. Boston: Houghton Mifflin Company, 1982.

Tayntor, Liz, Paul Erickson, and Les Kaufman. **Dive to the Coral Reefs.** New York: Crown Publishers, Inc., 1986.

Zeiller, Warren. **Tropical Marine Invertebrates of Southern Florida and the Bahama Islands,** 26. New York, London, Sydney, Toronto: John Wiley and Sons, 1974.

INDEX